THE PARENT AND CHILD
PROGRAMME

Marjorie's Ring

Shirley Isherwood

Illustrated by David Pross

To Parents

How to read this book together

- You, as the Storyteller, read the words at the bottom of each page.

- After you have read your part, ask your child to join in with the words in the speech bubbles, and point to the words as they are read.

Remember young children love repetition — it builds their confidence in reading. Always praise good guesses, and if your child is stuck just give the word yourself. This is far more helpful than sounding out individual letters.

The Riddlers of Riddleton End

Talk about the characters your child may have met in **The Riddlers** TV series. There's wise Mossop and his young friend Tiddler, who live at the bottom of the well in Marjorie Daw's garden, and have lots of adventures with Postie the hedgehog and Filbert the squirrel. The books also introduce some new characters — Harvest Mouse, Frog, The Dawn Fairy and a family of mischievous voles.

The Riddlers is a ❤ Yorkshire Television Production.

One day, a magpie stole
Marjorie's ring.

Tiddler saw him fly over the garden with the ring in his beak.

"I've got it! I've got it! I've got it!"
cried the magpie as he flew to his
nest in the tree.

7

Just then, Postie came through the gap in the hedge.

"The magpie's got Marjorie's ring," said Tiddler.
"I'll get it back," said Postie.

9

Postie began to climb the tree, but he only reached the first branch.

10

"I'm not very good at climbing trees," he said.
"I'll get it back," said Tiddler.

Tiddler began to climb the tree,
but she only reached the second
branch.
"I'm not very good at climbing
trees," she said.

Just then, Mossop came into
the garden.
"The magpie's got Marjorie's ring,"
said Tiddler.
"I'll get it back," said Mossop.

13

Mossop began to climb the tree, but he only reached the third branch. "I'm not very good at climbing trees," he said.

The magpie sat in his nest and
looked down at Mossop, Tiddler
and Postie.
"I've got it! I've got it! I've got it!"
he cried.

15

Just then, Harvest Mouse came into the garden. Postie saw her peeping through the blades of grass.

16

"The magpie's got Marjorie's ring,"
said Postie.
"I'll get it back," said Harvest Mouse.
But Harvest Mouse could only go a
little way up the trunk of the tree.

17

Just then, Frog came hopping
through the long grass.

"The magpie's got Marjorie's ring,"
said Harvest Mouse.
"I'll get it back," said Frog.
Frog tried to jump up to the nest,
but he couldn't jump high enough.

19

Just then, the family of voles came along the road. They had been for a picnic and were carrying their big picnic basket.

"The magpie's got Marjorie's ring,"
said Mossop.
"We'll get it back," said the voles.

21

The voles began to climb the tree.
The youngest ones reached the first
branch, their older brothers and
sisters reached the second branch,

22

and their mother and father, grandma
and grandpa reached the third
branch. But no one could climb up
to the magpie's nest to get the ring.

23

Just then, Filbert came into the
garden.
"Why are you all sitting in the
tree?" she asked.

"The magpie's got Marjorie's ring,"
said the voles, "and no one can
climb the tree."

"I'll get it back," said Filbert, and
she scampered right to the top of
the tree and got the ring.

"Poor magpie," said Tiddler. "He **does** like shiny things."

But the magpie didn't seem to
mind, for he had flown down from
the tree and was sitting on the edge
of the picnic basket.

28

In his beak was the shiny silver top
from the voles' milk bottle.

"I've got it! I've got it! I've got it!"
he cried, as he flew back to his nest.